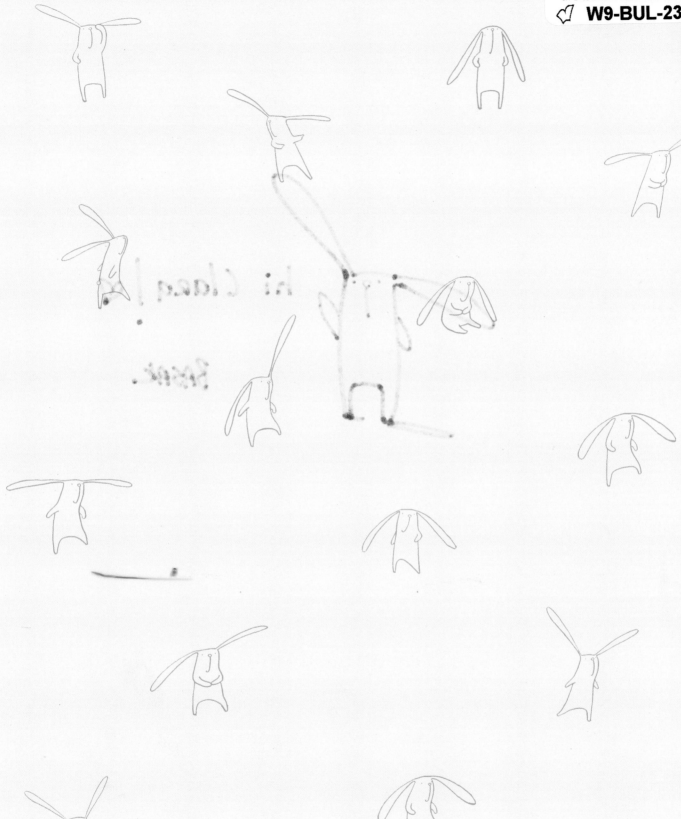

hi Clara! ♡

BASAK

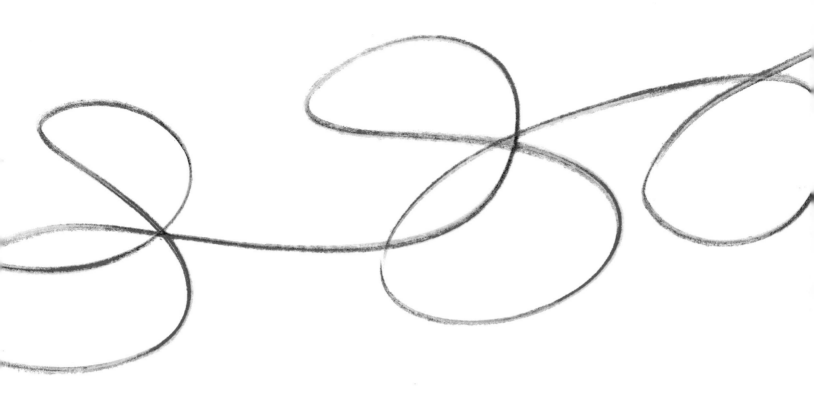

THE ALMOST IMPOSSIBLE THING

Philomel Books

Basak Agaoglu

Once upon a time
there was a dream,

a dream that tried to take shape.

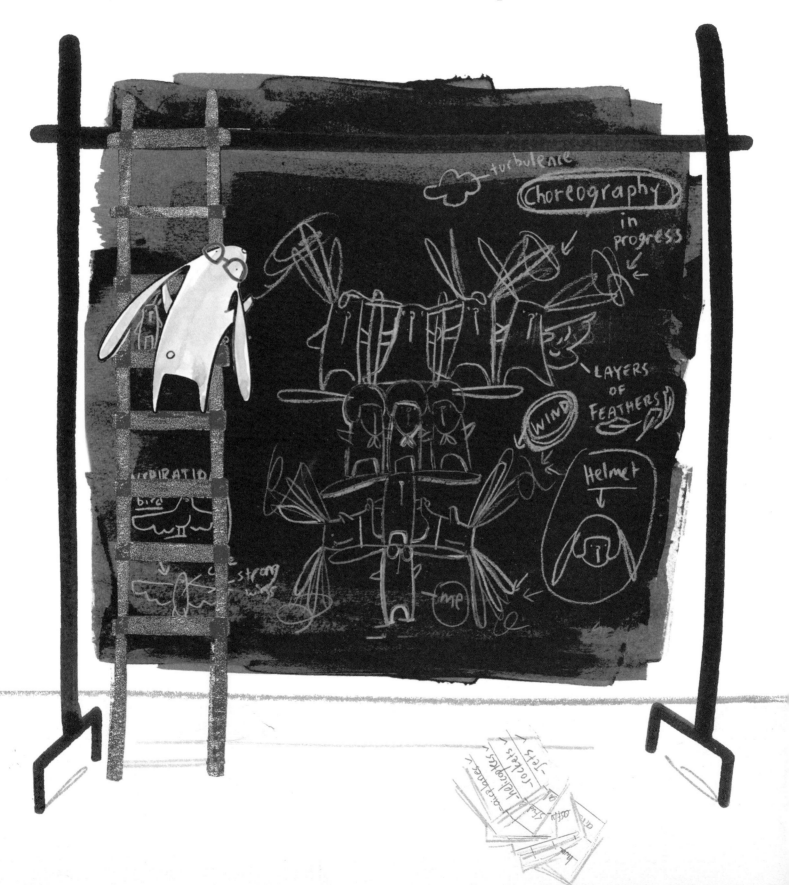

The dream didn't know
that it had no shape,

or that others
couldn't see it at all.

Unless it was kept in a tiny box.

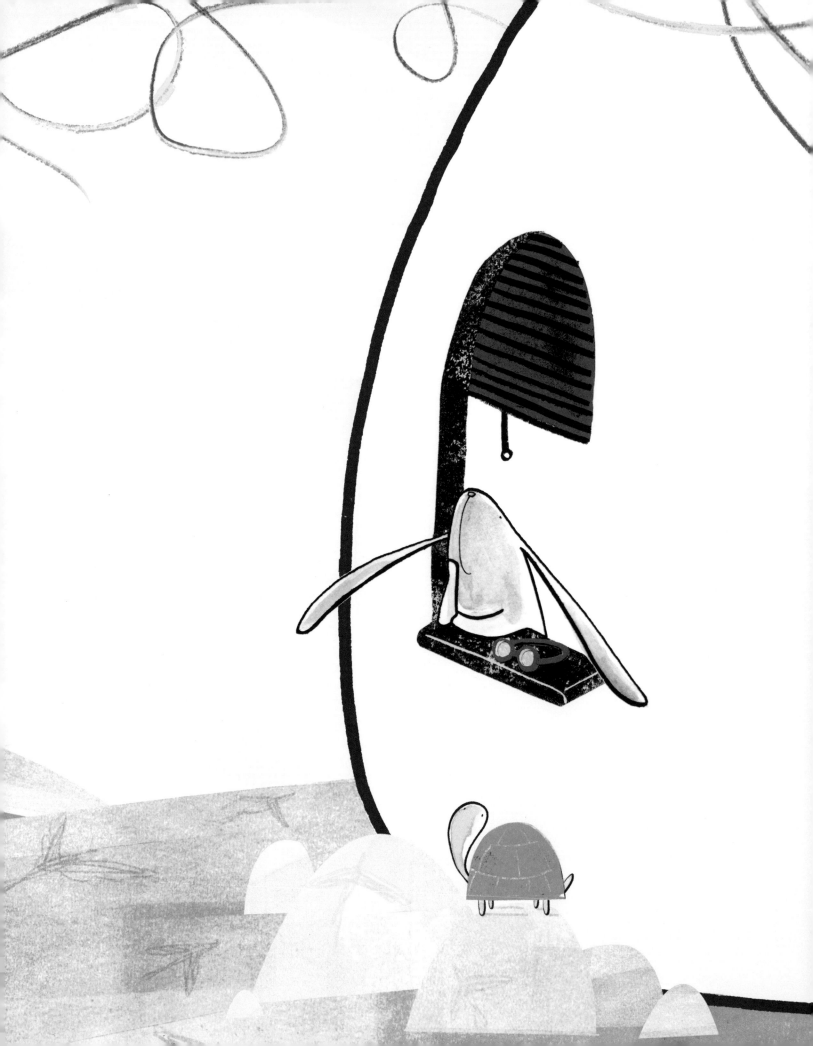

And never moved from its place
in the closet, where sunlight couldn't reach it.

The dream knew none of this.

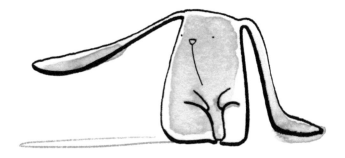

The dream knew only that it was too big for its home.

And too alive to sit in one place.

So it pulled

and it pushed.

And it pushed

and it pulled.

Until one day . . .

the power of that dream turned its box into . . .

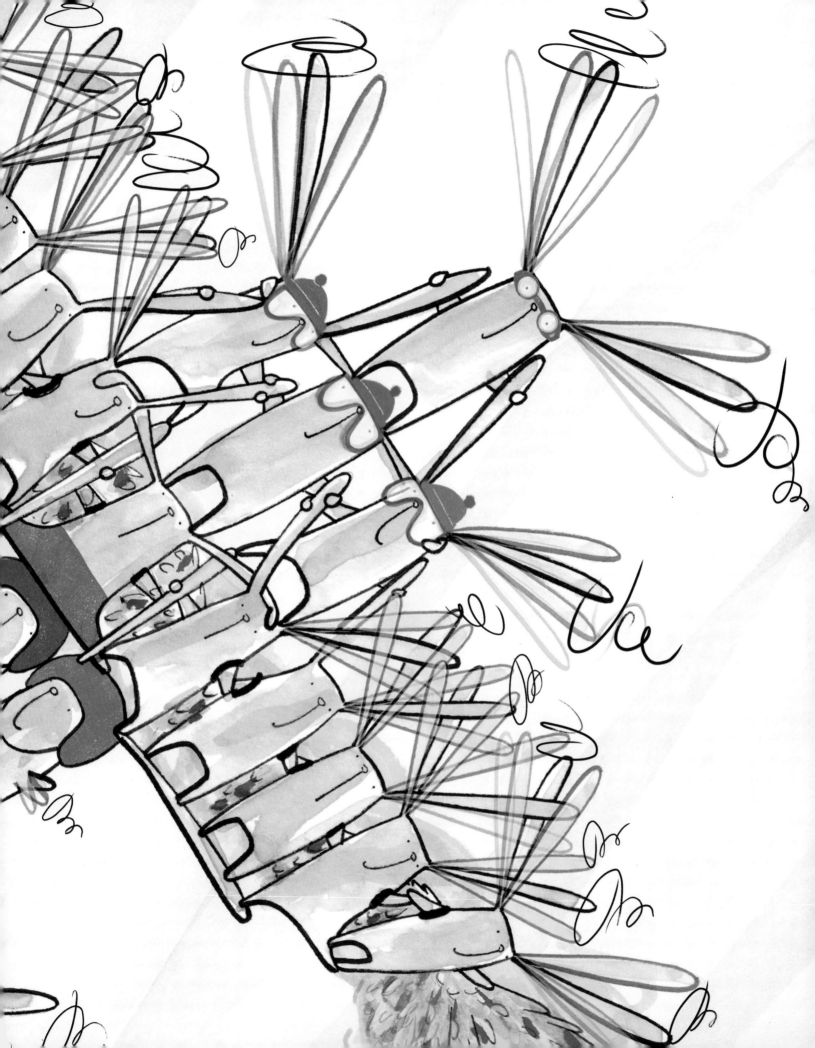

...a rocket ship that flew into the light. And sparkled with every color

that people could see.

And even a few that they couldn't.

For Asli, Ozcan and Can

PHILOMEL BOOKS
an imprint of Penguin Random House LLC
375 Hudson Street, New York, NY 10014

Library of Congress Cataloging-in-Publication Data is available upon request.
Manufactured in China by RR Donnelley Asia Printing Solutions Ltd.
ISBN 9780399548277
10 9 8 7 6 5 4 3 2 1

Edited by Michael Green.
Design by Ellice M. Lee & Jennifer Chung.
Text set in Archer.
The art was created with block printing, gouache and ink.